withdrawn

With love to all my family, especially Madeleine,
and with many thanks to Paul Dowswell – LA

For my brother Steven, with love.
Thanks go to my friends at the Lion & Unicorn,
The Pavilion and the lovely people at Scholastic – SH

First published in 2008
by Scholastic Children's Books
Euston House, 24 Eversholt Street
London NW1 1DB
a division of Scholastic Ltd
www.scholastic.co.uk
London ~ New York ~ Toronto ~ Sydney ~ Auckland
Mexico City ~ New Delhi ~ Hong Kong

HB ISBN 978 1407 10467 6
PB ISBN 978 1407 10468 3

Ordinary Oscar

Laura Adkins & Sam Hearn

SCHOLASTIC

In the **moonlit** garden of Number Six,
Crinkly Close, the snails are busy.
Slowly they **munch** and **crunch** the tasty,
tender leaves of potted plants
and juicy lettuces.
They are all **happy** snails.

Well, **nearly**
all of them...

Oscar Slimeglider
was **not** happy.
"I'm **tired** of sleeping
all day," he said.

"I'm **fed up** with
eating all night.

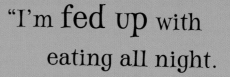

"I'm bored with being greenish-greyish-brownish.

"I want other snails to look at me and say, 'Wow! There's Oscar Slimeglider!'

"I want to be different...

"Nonsense!" frowned Oscar's dad.
"What's wrong with sleeping all day?
What's wrong with eating all night?"

"And what's wrong with being
greenish-greyish-brownish?" worried
Oscar's mum. "Your twenty-five brothers
and sisters never complain."

"We never complain!"

But Oscar was **determined**.
"The Wise Old Snail
will know what to do,"
he declared.

So off he went.

"What do you want
to be famous **for**?"
asked the Wise Old Snail.

"Can you paint?

"Can you dance?

"Can you play the guitar?"

Oscar shook his head.

"Being famous isn't **always** easy, you know," grumbled the Wise Old Snail. "Are you **sure** about this?"

Oscar nodded.

"Very well then," sighed the Wise Old Snail.

"You're going to need a bit of **magic**."

And he told Oscar what to do.

Oscar waited patiently
for the sun to rise.
Then he **turned** around
three times and cried,

*"Slime,
slime!
Slither,
slither!
Fairy
Godsnail,
please come
hither!"*

The **Fairy Godsnail** appeared.
"So you want to be famous?"
she smiled.
"Yes, please!"
Oscar wriggled eagerly.
"Then I shall grant you three wishes,"
replied the **Fairy Godsnail**.
"But choose carefully," she warned.

Then she waved her **magic wand**
and disappeared.

Oscar closed his eyes
tightly and made a **wish**...

Slowly, Oscar opened his eyes.
"Look at me!" he gasped.

"I'll be famous for being the most marvellous mollusc!

I'm a stunning, stupendous, spectacular snail! Everyone will admire me."

And sure enough, someone was admiring Oscar…

Up above, a **hungry** bird
smiled to himself.

"That snail looks like a
terrifically tasty treat,"
he thought, plunging down.

"Help!
Help!"

"Get your great
greedy beak **off** me
Oscar wailed.

"I wish I was
bigger than you –

"BIGGER!"

Oscar landed in town.

He was bigger than a bus,
bigger than six buses glued together.

"Call the police!"

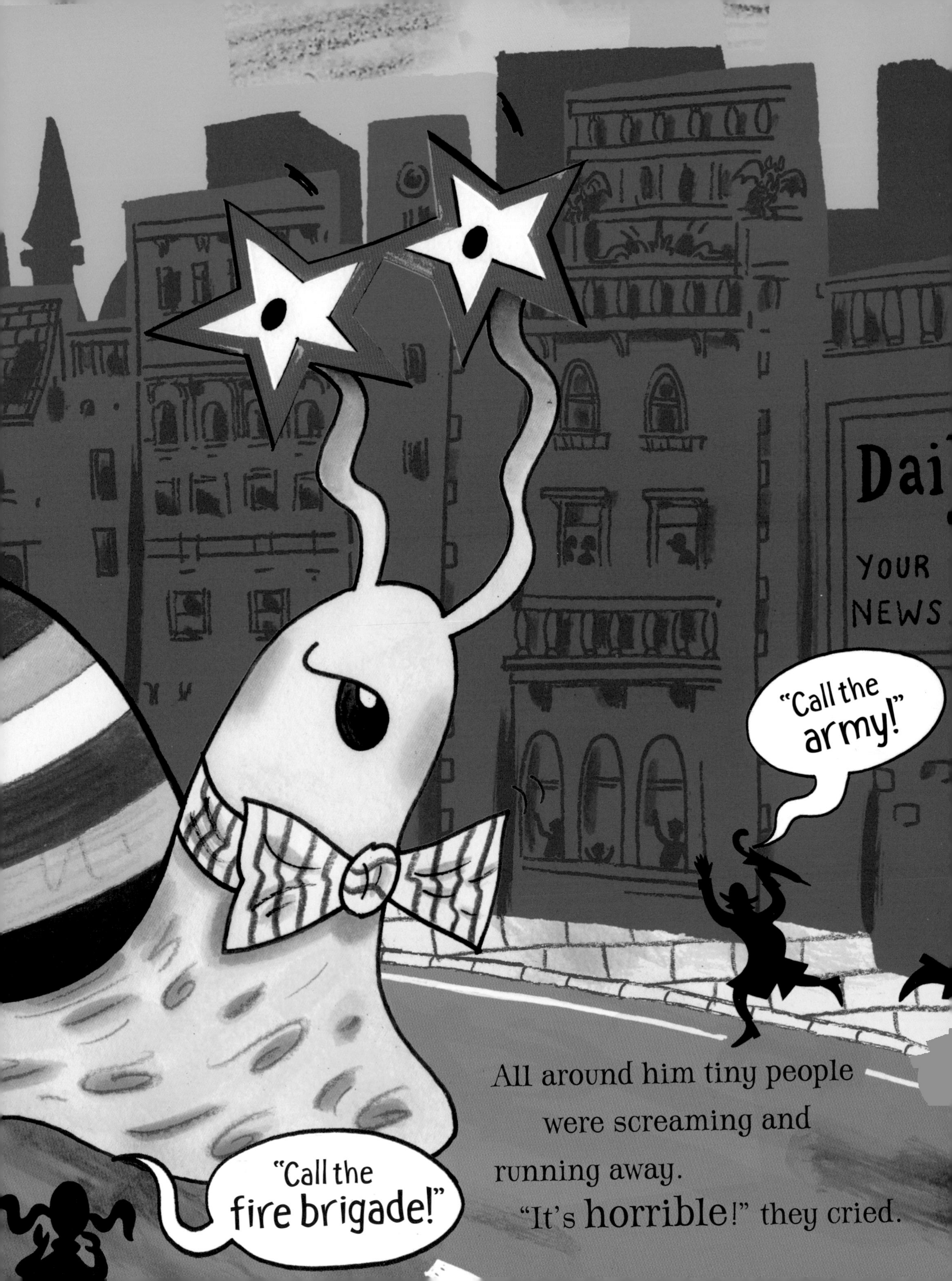
YOUR
NEWS
"Call the army!"
"Call the fire brigade!"

All around him tiny people were screaming and running away.

"It's **horrible**!" they cried.

As the sun began to sink,
Oscar slithered into the woods to hide.
"Now I'm famous for being frightening," he sniffed,
"and I have no friends."
Oscar began to cry.

"I want to go **home**
to Mum and Dad
and my twenty-five
brothers and sisters.
I wish I was
just **ordinary**
Oscar again."

And just like that…

…he was home.

"Where have you been, Oscar?"
asked his dad.
"We've been awfully worried about you."
"We thought you might
have been squashed!" said his mum.

"Now, it's dinner time. I've got some **tasty**, tender leaves, just for you."

"**Mmm**, my favourite," smiled Oscar. "Perhaps being **ordinary** isn't so bad after all."

But sometimes,
just sometimes, even
an ordinary snail can do
extraordinary things.

Six weeks later…

THAT'S MY BOY

By **Mike Mollusc**
Garden Correspondent

Shellebrity: Mrs Slimeglider looks on proudly at her heroic son

COMPETITION : Win a copy of

Snail

www.dailysnail.sl.ime

70 Leaves

When Mrs Gertrude Slimeglider fell into some shifting soil, she was overcome by panic.

For Gertrude – who is expecting 60 eggs next week – was trapped, while her twenty-six children, Agnes, Bernard, Cornelius, Destiny, Electra, Fifi, Georgina, Heathcliff, Ingrid, Jethro, Keanu, Lavender, Mozart, Norbert, Oscar, Pandora, Quentin, Rupert, Sigmund, Thomas, Ursula, Veronica, Wilma, Xavier, Yeats and Zebedee roamed the flower bed. "I told Agnes to go and fetch her dad, but because he was so far away I knew that would take a long time."

With her husband on the other side of the garden Gertrude was desperate, until clever Oscar came to the rescue.

"He's a very sensible and caring snail"

Anxious Oscar, a St Mollusc pupil, had gathered all his siblings together. Under his direction they began to eat the surrounding plants. The brave youngster kept his cool and soon the soil began to shift, allowing Gertrude to escape.

"He's a very sensible and caring snail. He knew I was expecting eggs and I think that made him more aware of the situation. I'm really proud of him," said Gertrude.

"When my husband gets here and hears about what happened, I know he'll be proud too," she added.

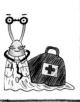

t Composters: *A History Of Music* by W.O. Snail ✳ Call 0800 S-N-A-I-L ✳

The End